A FOX
GOT MY SOCKS

For Charlie Everton Bingham

A Red Fox Book

Published by Random House Children's Books
20 Vauxhall Bridge Road, London SW1V 2SA

A division of Random House UK Ltd
London Melbourne Sydney Auckland
Johannesburg and agencies throughout the world

First published in 1992 by Hutchinson Children's Books

Red Fox edition 1994

Designed by Paul Welti

Printed in China

RANDOM HOUSE UK Limited Reg. No. 954009

ISBN 0 09 999780 0

A FOX
GOT MY SOCKS
Hilda Offen

RED FOX

Yesterday
was washing day.

Pretend to wash

My clothes flip-flapped
and blew away.

Flap arms

A cat got my hat.

Touch head with both hands

A fox got my socks.

Touch both feet

A goat got my coat.

Pretend to do up buttons

An owl got my towel.

Pretend to flap towel

'Oh no!' said the pig.
'These pants are too big!'

Pretend to hold up pants

And the bear gave a snort:
'This jumper's too short!'

Pull jumper up

Two baby llamas
were in my pyjamas

Touch chest and knee

And where was my scarf?
Wrapped round a giraffe!

Pretend to wrap scarf

But the sun was so hot,

Fan face

I said, 'Keep what you've got.

Hold out arms

I'm perfectly happy ...

... to stay in my nappy!' *Dance around*

Some bestselling Red Fox picture books

THE BIG ALFIE AND ANNIE ROSE STORYBOOK
by Shirley Hughes
OLD BEAR
by Jane Hissey
OI! GET OFF OUR TRAIN
by John Burningham
DON'T DO THAT!
by Tony Ross
NOT NOW, BERNARD
by David McKee
ALL JOIN IN
by Quentin Blake
THE MOON'S REVENGE
by Joan Aiken and Alan Lee
BAD BORIS GOES TO SCHOOL
by Susie Jenkin-Pearce
WE CAN SAY NO!
by David Pithers and Sarah Greene
MATILDA
by Hilaire Belloc and Posy Simmonds
WILLY AND HUGH
by Anthony Browne
THE WINTER HEDGEHOG
by Ann and Reg Cartwright
A DARK, DARK TALE
by Ruth Brown
HARRY, THE DIRTY DOG
by Gene Zion and Margaret Bloy Graham
DR XARGLE'S BOOK OF EARTHLETS
by Jeanne Willis and Tony Ross
JAKE
by Deborah King